# Hunter's Secret

by Kate Mead
illustrated by Stephen Axelsen

SCHOOL PUBLISHERS

Printed in Mexico

ISBN 10: 0-15-351425-6
ISBN 13: 978-0-15-351425-8

Ordering Options
ISBN 10: 0-15-351212-1 (Grade 2 Advanced Collection)
ISBN 13: 978-0-15-351212-4 (Grade 2 Advanced Collection)
ISBN 10: 0-15-358060-7 (package of 5)
ISBN 13: 978-0-15-358060-4 (package of 5)

1 2 3 4 5 6 7 8 9 10   050   15 14 13 12 11 10 09 08 07 06

The students at Featherston School were holding a talent show to raise money for the school library.

"I'm going to do a magic trick," announced Marvin right away.

Hunter looked glum. He didn't know any magic tricks.

The students in Hunter's class discussed what they could do at the talent show to entertain people. The teacher wrote their ideas on the whiteboard until it was covered.

All the children were excited, except Hunter. Everyone but Hunter had thought of something to do for the talent show, so they all tried to help him.

"I'll give you dancing lessons, and then you can dance with me," said Anna.

    During Hunter's dance classes, Anna moved around as carefree as a butterfly. Hunter stomped behind her with heavy steps. His feet did not bounce up and down like Anna's when he danced. Hunter decided not to dance with Anna at the talent show.

"Try singing with me," suggested Alex.

Hunter tried singing, but when he tried to reach the high notes, he sounded like a screeching bird. He decided not to sing at the talent show.

Over the weekend, Hunter discussed the show with his mom. "I don't know what to do for the talent show," he said gloomily. "I can't sing or dance or do anything else."

"Yes, you can," his mom said as she
sipped her coffee. "Everyone is good at
something. You just need to find out
what you're good at doing," she said.

Hunter thought carefully about what
his mom had said. After a few minutes,
an idea for the talent show had already
popped into his head.

On the night of the talent show, Anna was the first to perform. Some dancers came next, followed by a song from Alex.

The people in the audience clapped for each performance. They also stomped and cheered to show their support.

Last to perform was Hunter. He
walked onto the stage with a large book
in one hand and a wooden stool in the
other. The lights on the stage went down,
and a spotlight beamed down on him.

Hunter sat on the stool, opened the large book, and started to read aloud. Everyone listened carefully to Hunter. Sometimes they laughed, and sometimes they sat in silence.

When Hunter finished, he shut his book, picked up his stool, and left the stage. Everyone stood and clapped for a long time.

After Hunter's performance, the children gathered round Hunter backstage.

"You kept that a secret," laughed Anna.

"You were fantastic!' said Alex.

"We all have different things we can do," said Hunter. "I'm glad I am good at storytelling."

They all agreed that he was.

# Think Critically

1. Why were the students at Featherston School holding the talent show?

2. Where was Hunter when he came up with his good idea?

3. How did Hunter feel at the end of the story compared to how he felt at the beginning?

4. What words would you use to describe Hunter's friends?

5. If you were in a talent show, what would you do? Why?

 **Social Studies**

**Write a Paragraph** Hunter's friends tried to help him learn what he was good at doing. Write a paragraph about a time when somebody helped you learn something.

**School-Home Connection** Tell a family member about *Hunter's Secret.* Then talk about a time you performed in front of an audience.